Deep-Sea Disaster

SHARK SCHOOL

Deep-Sea Disaster

BY DAVY OCEAN
ILLUSTRATED BY AARON BLECHA

SCHOLASTIC INC.

WiTH THANKS TO PAUL EBBS

Originally published in Great Britain in 2013 by Templar Publishing

ISBN 978-0-545-81836-0

12 11 10 9 8 7 6 5 4 3 2 1   15 16 17 18 19 20/0

Printed in China   68

This edition first printing, January 2015

Cover designed by Karin Paprocki
Interior designed by Mike Rosamilia
The text of this book was set in Write Demibd.

CHAPTER 1

I'm having my favorite dream again—
the one where I'm about to be crowned
Greatest Underwater Wrestling Champion of the World, Ever. I swim up to
the top rope of the ring and prepare to
launch.

"I think he's going for a dropflick!"

a jellyfish commentator shouts into his microphone.

"There's no stopping this hammer-head shark tonight," adds his partner, a bright orange clown fish.

"Har-ry! Har-ry!" the crowd begins to chant.

One diving dropflick and the blue shark I'm fighting will be fish food and the underwater wrestling belt will be mine. I dive down from the rope and pin my opponent to the canvas.

"Har-ry! Har-ry!" The crowd's voices get louder and louder. And louder. And then too loud. Like they are shouting right in my ear.

"HARRY—GET OFF!"

I open my left eye and swivel it around. The wrestling ring disappears and I am in my bedroom. Next to my bed. And Humphrey, my humming-fish alarm clock, is pinned to the floor under me.

"Let me go!" he yells.

"All right, all right," I mutter, swimming

back into bed. "Why did you have to wake me up? I was having a really cool dream."

"Don't tell me, the one about the wrestling match?" Humphrey says grumpily.

"Yes."

"I hate that dream."

"Why?"

"I always end up getting hurt."

I open my right eye and glare at him. "Only because you try to wake me up."

Humphrey starts swimming around in circles above my head. "It's my job to wake you up—I'm your alarm clock, and you've got school."

I groan. From almost being crowned

4

Underwater Wrestling Champion of the World to having to get ready for school, in less than ten seconds.

"So, are you awake, then?"

"Yes!"

"Cool. See you tomorrow."

"Can't wait."

Humphrey swims off out the window to go and get his breakfast.

I swivel my right eye around until I can see the huge poster of Gregor the Gnasher hanging on the rocky wall at the end of my bed. Gregor the Gnasher is the *actual* Underwater Wrestling Champion of the World. In the poster, he's holding his winner's belt high above his head and smiling so widely you can see all of his 3,017 teeth.

Gregor is a great white shark and as well as his rows and rows of razor-sharp teeth, he has a long pointed snout and a humongous body. He's exactly what a shark *should* look like. And he's scary. Super scary. Even my poster of him makes my pet catfish poop itself.

If they made a poster of me, my catfish would probably just laugh. You see, I'm a hammerhead shark, which, for those of you who haven't already figured it out,

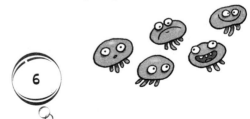

means I have a head that's the shape of a hammer. With goggly eyes so far apart they look like they don't even talk to each other. It's not a great look. Espe-

cially if you want to be taken seriously in the shark world.

I once made a list of the five coolest sharks in existence. It went like this:

1. The great white—obviously.

2. The blue shark—
the fastest fish in
the sea.

3. The tiger shark—
scary and stripy.

4. The whale shark—
its mouth is so huge
it can swallow a
dolphin in one gulp!

5. The bull shark—
it can swim in
rivers as well as
the sea. which is
very handy if you're
going on vacation and stuff.

ROAR.

You may have noticed that the hammer-head shark isn't on the list. That's because the hammerhead shark is seriously uncool. In fact, the only shark less cool than a hammer-head is the nurse shark. Nurse sharks are the girliest sharks in the ocean—which is fine if you're a girl and everything, but I'm not.

Gregor doesn't just look cool, he can do lots of cool stuff too. Then I have an idea. I might not look like Gregor, but that doesn't mean I can't *be* like him. I swim out of bed and over to the old treasure chest where I keep my collec-tion of shells shaped like famous sports stars and all my lists. I once made a list of all the cool stuff Gregor can do. I take it out and study it.

Number one is out, obviously.

1. Wrestling—he's the Underwater Champion ten years running.

2. Eating boats—which scares the life out of the leggy air-breathers.

3. Looking really mean—without even trying.

4. Swimming fast—as fast as any speedboat.

5. Ambushing prey—they never see him coming.

You can't just be Underwater Wrestling Champion of the World in, like, two weeks or something. It takes years of deep-sea training: weight-lifting anchors, eating high-energy seaweed bars, and swimming laps around ocean liners.

Number two is a no-no as well. First of all, my mouth is way too small. Sometimes I find it hard swallowing a crab. Also, I'm not allowed up to the surface without one of my parents being with me. I know that sounds really lame—I mean, I'm ten years old. What do they think I'm going to do? Go sunbathing on the beach?

And I'm not going to eat any strange food dangling from fishing lines either. Everyone knows what fishermen do to sharks when they catch them. They make their fins into soup, that's what. And there's no way I'd risk losing my fins. Imagine what a laughingstock I'd be then, with a head like a hammer and a body like an eel!

I put on my school tie and blazer and then read number three on my list: *Looking really mean.* Hmm, now that sounds a bit easier. And if I looked really mean, certain sharks might not make fun of me anymore. I swim over to my mirror and scrunch my eyes shut. Then I make my meanest face. I imagine I'm giving the sort of scary scowl that Gregor makes when he's entering the wrestling ring. It feels pretty good. I can already imagine Rick Reef and his goofy sidekick, Donny Dogfish, taking one look at the new me and speeding off to hide behind the school cafeteria.

But when I open my eyes and look in the mirror, I don't see the mean monster of my dreams—and Rick Reef's nightmares—I see a schoolkid who looks like he's having trouble making a poop!

I swim back to the list, feeling a bit worried. I'm starting to run out of options. Okay, number four: *Swimming fast.* I'm not bad at this, actually, but I'm not clueless—I'm never going to be as fast as Gregor. I look at number five: *Ambushing prey.* Aha—now, surely I can do that. I mean, how hard can it be? I scan my bedroom, looking for a victim. My eyes come to rest upon Lenny, my lantern fish, snoozing away above my desk, his antennae glowing softly in the dark. Being careful not to make a sound, I start to glide through the water, Gregor's scary theme song playing in my head.

DERRRRRRR-DUN! DERRRRRR-DUN! DER-DUN! DER-DUN! DER-DUN! DER-DUN!

But just as I get to the desk, disaster strikes. My tail gets caught in a strand from my seaweed blanket. I try to tug it free but end up getting even more tangled. I pull as hard as I can. The balled-up blanket sails through the water, hits the shelf above my bed, and sends my finball trophy flying.

"Eh? Uh! Wass going on?" Lenny says sleepily as I try to untangle myself from the seaweed.

Hmm, not exactly the kind of surprise

attack I'd been planning. But the problem is, my room's way too small. You can't really sneak up on something when it's really close to begin with. You need a little distance from the target to be able to plan your attack. I decide to investigate the rest of the house to see what I can find.

But as I swim through my bedroom door, I hear a really horrible noise. It's like a crab grinding glass with its pincers. Or a ship's foghorn that has a seagull stuck inside it. It can only be one thing—my mom, singing while she makes breakfast. I start to grin. When

Mom is singing, she goes off into her own little world and doesn't notice a thing. She will make the perfect target. Let the ambushing begin!

While Mom keeps screeching like a harpooned mermaid, I get to the kitchen door without being seen. Then I poke one side of my hammerhead through the door and swivel my eye around, trying to spot my prey. There she is, at the far end of the kitchen, putting breakfast things on a tray, still singing away. Now that I'm closer I can actually make out some of the words in between the screeches:

"Like an anchor—dropped for the very first time. Like an a-a-a-anchor . . ."

Oh, please!

I slink my way into the room and slide behind the giant glass vase of flower fish in the corner. Honestly, I don't know why we can't just have regular sea flowers like everyone else. It was my dad's idea of a joke. But the trouble is, my dad's idea of a joke isn't ever anybody else's idea of a joke. I don't know how he managed to get elected as the new Shark Point mayor.

I get myself ready to pounce. *This must be how Gregor feels before a fight,* I think as my heart starts to pound.

I hear my unsuspecting prey swimming for the door, her apron strings swishing in the water behind her. Closer and closer she comes.

"Made of iron, shiny and fine," she wails.

I tense my muscles. Closer she comes. I arch my back. And closer. I get ready to pounce. Closer. NOW!

CHAPTER 2

Okay, I'll admit it, the ambush didn't go 100 percent according to plan. It went about 10 percent according to plan. The surprise part worked great—that was the 10 percent—but what happened right after wasn't so good. The chain of events went like this:

1. I leaped out from behind the flower fish, yelling at the top of my lungs . . .

2. Mom screeched—and this time she wasn't singing . . .

3. Mom dropped the breakfast tray . . .

4. I smashed into it . . .

5. And sent everything flying EVERYWHERE.

And now everything has gone dark on one side of the room. I swivel my right eye but can't see anything out of it. My ambush has turned into a terrible tragedy!

"I'm blind! I'm blind!" I cry.

Mom stops screaming. "Breakfast bowl," she gasps, pointing a shaking fin at me.

I blink my working eye at her in disbelief. Why is she calling me breakfast bowl? Has my ambush made her go crazy? And why isn't she looking more concerned? Her only son has just told her he can't see anymore! From one eye, at least.

"What?" I say.

"Breakfast bowl."

"Why do you keep calling me that?" I yell. "I've gone blind in one eye."

"It's a breakfast bowl," she squeals.

"What are you talking about?" I start to panic. I have gone blind and my mom has gone crazy. So far this is not turning out to be a very good morning.

"You've got a breakfast bowl over your eye," Mom explains.

I shake my head and, sure enough, a bowl falls off and drifts to the floor, leaving Kelp Krispies trickling down my face. Although I'm relieved I'm not actually blind and my mom isn't actually crazy, I can't help thinking sadly that this would never, ever happen to Gregor the Gnasher.

"What in the name of all the oceans were you doing, Harry?" Mom asks.

"Sorry, Mom," I reply, looking at the floor. "I was only trying to ambush you."

"Only trying to ambush me!" Mom echoes, wiping the Kelp Krispies off my head with the bottom of her apron. (I bet that's never happened to Gregor either!) "Hammerheads don't ambush things, you silly little starfish!"

I cringe with embarrassment. How

am I ever going to be taken as seriously as a great white when my mom calls me names like that? "I was trying to be like Gregor the Gnasher," I try to explain.

Mom sighs. "I'll never understand why you kids think that tooth-head is some kind of hero."

"Hero? Did someone say hero?" my dad booms, entering the kitchen. "Well, here I am! Ha, ha, ha!"

I told you his jokes weren't funny.

"Oh, you'll always be our hero, darling," laughs Mom, before giving him a massive kiss.

I think I might be sick. There's only so much a ten-year-old hammerhead can take in one morning.

"What was all that noise about?" Dad asks. He looks around at the mess. "And why's my breakfast on the floor?"

To stop Mom from going through the whole ambush disaster again, I decide to change the conversation.

"How's the speech going, Dad?"

My dad's working on his first ever speech as mayor. Most of Shark Point will be there to hear it, so I hope he doesn't tell any jokes.

"It's going great," Dad replies, "but I think I should start with a joke. Better yet, maybe two jokes. . . . "

Where's a fisherman's hook when you need one?

"How about this one?" says Dad as Mom starts picking up the plates and bowls from the floor. "What do you call a fish with no eyes?"

I stare at him and shake my head. "I dunno."

"A fsh!" he replies, before roaring with laughter. "Get it? No *i*'s. Ha ha ha!"

He sees me staring at him, not laughing. "Okay, well, maybe I'll think of a different joke. I'll be in the living room." And with that, he turns and swims back down the hall.

"Honey, can you turn on your hammer--vision and see if you can find the lid for the teapot while I clean up?" Mom asks. "I must have dropped it in your . . . ambush."

I turn on the special sensors in my head and start swimming around the kitchen. Having sensors is like having a bunch of extra eyes that can see inside and through things. And because our heads are so big, hammerheads have the most powerful sensors in the entire ocean. It's pretty cool. Especially if you want to find out where your parents have hidden your Christmas presents. Mom goes crazy when I do this. She says the reason we have sensors is so that we can find food even if it's buried deep beneath the sea-bed. She says that using our sensors to find hidden presents is wrong. But then, she would say that—she's a parent. As far as parents are concerned, everything that's fun is "wrong"!

I find the teapot lid right away—behind a sea cucumber on the table.

"Thank you, dear," Mom says as I give it to her. "You've certainly got excellent hammer-vision—and it's so much more useful than ambushing. I mean, who needs to hunt for prey these days, when you can just go to the supermarket?"

"But ambushing's exciting and cool," I reply. "When I use my sensors, I'm just . . . trying to find stuff."

"What is cool," says Mom, "is your class outing to the *Titan* today. So you'd better get some breakfast inside you or you're going to be late."

The *Titan*! I'd completely forgotten about the school trip to the shipwreck. It wasn't as exciting as going out to the deep ocean to see great whites—but it was a day out of school.

I barely manage to cram down some breakfast before I hear Ralph shouting for me outside. Ralph is a pilot fish and one of my best friends.

I grab my backpack and head for the door.

"Bye, Mom. Bye, Dad."

"Bye, angelfish!" Mom calls.

"Bye, son," Dad hollers. "What kind of fish feels the most pain?"

I pretend not to hear him.

"A sore-dine! Ha, ha, ha!"

My parents are so embarrassing!

Outside, Ralph is swimming around our front yard, his silver stripes glinting in the sunshine.

"Hey, Harry, all ready for the school trip?" he says as soon as he sees me.

"You bet," I reply.

"So what did you have for breakfast today?" he asks.

"Shrimp Pop-Tarts."

"Cool, my favorite. Okay then, open wide, I'm going in!"

I open my mouth as wide as I can and Ralph dives in and starts nibbling at my teeth.

This is what pilot fish do, by the way—they eat the scraps of food from between sharks' teeth. They're kind of like swimming, talking toothbrushes.

As soon as Ralph has finished we start making our way toward the center of town.

We've just reached the water park when Joe shows up. Joe is a bright yellow jellyfish and another one of my friends. One of the coolest things about Joe is that he has a bunch of arms. Well, a *lot* of arms. The only uncool thing about Joe's arms is that it can take a *long* time to high-fin. I like him a lot, but he can be a worrier.

"Good morning, Joe," I say.

"Is it?" Joe replies.

Ralph and I stare at him.

"Of course it is—we're going on the trip to the *Titan*," says Ralph.

"Aren't you looking forward to it?" I ask.

"Not really," says Joe. "I'll probably get my tentacles trapped in a porthole, or be harpooned by a diver. Or lose my packed lunch in the wreckage, or—"

"Okay, okay, we get the point," says Ralph.

Joe's yellow tentacles quiver. "Why can't we just stay in school? It's much safer."

"Oh, come on, Joe," I say. "It'll be good to see more of the ocean."

"Why?" he replies. "It's all the same—just a lot of wet."

You can't really argue with that, so we stop at the stores and look in Seahorse Sports and Leisure to check out the latest games. Then we make our way to school. My heart sinks as I see Rick Reef and Donny Dogfish by the gates. Rick is a blacktip reef shark, which means he has this really cool black tip on his dorsal fin. He is wearing his matching black leather jacket (as usual) and showing off (as usual) by swimming really quickly through all the groups of kids. Donny is cheering him on (as usual), doing a sports commentary as Rick speeds around.

"And Rick Reef takes a sharp right past some second-grade clown fish and a left through a group of first-grade dolphins. See them scatter as the swimming captain speeds down the lane."

Rick is the school swimming captain and loves to let everyone know it.

Suddenly Rick spots our group and swims straight for us, pulling up at the last minute and showering us with air bubbles.

"Well, if it isn't old Anchor Face," he says.

"Good one, Rick," says Donny, smirking away beside him.

"Oh, grow up, Rick," says Ralph.

"Be quiet, Toothpick," says Rick. Then he turns to Joe. "Oh look, it's Jelly Belly."

Donny is almost dying laughing, but before anyone can say anything else, the school bell rings.

"Last one in's a sea snail," shouts Rick as he swims for the door.

I'll show him who's a sea snail, I think as I charge after him.

"What are you doing?" Ralph cries.

"Be careful," Joe calls. "You might sprain your tail or pull a fin muscle."

But I don't care. Nothing and no one is going to stop me. I'm going to teach that reef shark show-off a lesson. He might be the fastest swimmer in the school, but I have surprise on my side. Rick thinks no one would actually bother racing him because he's the swimming captain, so he isn't going that fast. I zoom past him into the school.

I speed along the corridor. The

classroom door is getting closer and closer. I swivel my left eye backward and see that Rick's gaining on me.

DERRRRRRR-DUN! DERRRRRR-DUN! DER-DUN! DER-DUN! DER-DUN! DER-DUN!

I think of Gregor the Gnasher's theme song and make a desperate lunge for the door.

DERRRRRRR-DUN! DERRRRRR-DUN! DER

"Ow!"

I'm so busy keeping one eye on Rick, I forget that the doorway is kind of narrow and go slamming straight into it. I desperately flail my tail, but it's no good. I'm stuck—my humongous hammerhead wedged in the door.

"Hey, Harry," I hear Rick tease from behind me, chuckling, "I've heard of getting something in your eye—but a whole door frame?"

KNOW YOUR
ANCHOVY
BARRACUDA
CATFISH

The entire class starts laughing their heads off. And they are still laughing as Ralph and Joe help me unwedge myself. I've never felt more embarrassed as I slink over to my desk.

But it had felt so good when I was actually beating Rick in the race. I decide then and there that I don't care what it takes, I'm going to prove I'm just as good as the rest of them. I'm going to show them all what a hammerhead can do!

CHAPTER 3

Creeeeeeeeeeeeeeeeaaaaaaaaaak!!!

At first I think the noise is coming from the rotting planks of the *Titan*. *Creeeeeeeeeeeeee-ak-ak-ak-ak-ak!!!*

But it isn't the *Titan*.

It's Joe's backside.

Ralph and I give him a look.

"Well, it is a bit scary!" Joe says, turning from bright yellow to bright pink with embarrassment.

And to be honest, Joe is right. It *is* scary.

As Mrs. Shelby, our sea-turtle teacher, leads us closer to the *Titan*, the butter-flies start to flap in my tummy too. The

wreck looms out of the green deep-sea gloom, dripping with seaweed and rust. The dark portholes along the side are like rows of spooky eyes staring at us. They make me want to shiver. But I'm not going to show that I'm scared, not with Rick and Donny hanging at the back of the line chewing sea gum and blowing bubbles. And besides, Gregor the Gnasher wouldn't be scared of an old shipwreck. No way.

Mrs. Shelby brings us to a halt beneath the enormous prow of the *Titan*. It towers over us like a cliff.

"Now, class," Mrs. Shelby says, peering

over her little round glasses. The shadow from the shipwreck has made her face dark. "Under no circumstances are you to go into the wreck. It is very, very dangerous in there. The *Titan* has been on the seabed for over a hundred years, and is rusting and rotting away. It could collapse at any moment and turn you into fish paste!"

Everyone giggles, until we see the serious look on Mrs. Shelby's face.

"I mean it. You're here to look at the area around the *Titan* for your geography project." Mrs. Shelby begins handing out round, flat pieces of rock with writing. "Here is a list of everything I want you to find."

Now, normally I love lists, but not this one.

1. A barnacle—boring!
2. Three different types of shell—more boring!
3. At least three colors of seaweed—I'm seriously starting to fall asleep now.
4. Zzzzzzzzzzzzzzzzzzzzzzz—see?

Ralph fins me in the side to wake me up.

"Once you've found everything on your checklist, meet back here, under the prow, okay?" Mrs. Shelby calls.

We all nod and start to swish away.

"Wait!"

We all stop.

"I need to put you in your groups."

Mrs. Shelby has a thing about us working in groups. It's really annoying. Doesn't she realize that I'm a shark, a lone hunter of the waves? I bet Gregor never gets put in a group. When she first starts reading the names of my group, it isn't too bad.

1. Me.
2. Joe—Yay!
3. Ralph—Double yay!
4. Donny—Boooooo!
5. Rick—Double boooooo! with extra boooooo! on the side and sprinkled with grated boooooo!

"Now, don't forget what I told you," Mrs. Shelby yells as we start to swim off. "No going inside the *Titan*—UNDER ANY CIRCUMSTANCES!"

"Yes, Mrs. Shelby," we all mutter.

Of course Rick immediately takes the lead in our group and decides which way we swim. We all follow him around to the collapsed stern of the *Titan*. It must have hit the seabed with a massive crunch. The whole back of the ship with its enormous propeller is ripped open and we can see right inside. The decks are layered like Mom's coral cake, and great piles of stuff like bed frames and chairs and doors and ladders have all fallen out onto the seabed in a big fan-shaped mess. It's starting to get covered in seaweed and barnacles and coral—it won't be long before the whole thing turns into a new reef. And Rick is leading us straight into it!

I look around but can only see the back of Mrs. Shelby's shell as she comforts Penny Puffer-Fish. Penny has gotten all spiky. Puffer fish only get spiky when they are very afraid and think they are about to die. Penny must be *very* scared of the *Titan.*

"Rick!" I call as loudly as I dare. "You heard what Mrs. Shelby said."

Rick looks back, smirks, and says, "I thought you were a hammerhead, not a scaredy-catfish. Donny and I are going into the wreck, 'cause that's where all the best barnacles are, and we're going to have the best project. Are you coming, or are you going to stay there making bubbles with your rears?"

Donny and Rick slap fins and swoosh off, right toward the hole in the back of the *Titan*.

Well, I'm not going to stand for that. "Come on, guys, let's go!" I cry.

"Where?" Ralph and Joe say together.

"With them!" I shout, pointing after Rick and Donny. I can see that Ralph isn't sure, and Joe is actually trying to hide under himself.

"It'll be fine," I say.

"Yeah, if 'FINE' stands for 'we'll be **F**ish food, **I**f **N**ot **E**xterminated,'" Joe mutters from beneath his tentacles.

With a bit of pushing and pulling, Ralph and I and, finally, Joe, head off toward the wreck.

Rick and Donny have already disappeared by the time we get to the massive hole in the back of the ship. Jagged strips of metal hang above us as sharp as razor shells. Thick, waterlogged beams of wood ripped from floors and walls look splintery and deadly.

"It feels colder. Does it feel colder to you?" Joe says with a shiver. "I'm turning from a jellyfish into an ice pop. I'm going to freeze and die. I've already lost the feeling in my seventh tentacle!"

Ralph swims up to me with a barnacle in his fins. "Got one—let's go," he
says with a tremble in his voice.

I'm just about to agree when some
stuff happens. Stuff that means I'm not
leaving the wreck. Well, not yet.

The stuff that happens is:

1. Rick appears with

    a big, toothy grin.

2. Donny arrives too

    (but he doesn't look as grinny.

    In fact, he looks a bit sick to his stomach).

3. Rick flubbers the side of my hammer

    with his fin.

4. **Flubbering** the side of my hammer with his fin
   makes my stupid rubbery head **boing** about and
   makes my words come out all **flibbery**.

5. "D-d-d-d-d-d-don't
   d-d-d-d-d-d-d-do
   d-d-d-d-d-d-d-dat!"

See?

Luckily, Ralph and Joe know what
to do. They each catch an end of my
head and hold on tightly until it stops
flibber-flabbering.

"Come on, Rubberhead," Rick says,
"look what we've found!"

I hate it when Rick flubbers my head.

Hammerheads are the only sharks you can do it to, and he does it all the time. It makes me feel dorkey. Well, I'm not going to let him see me scared, too!

With one kick of my tail, I follow, and since Ralph and Joe are still holding on to my head, they come too.

As I swim on into the *Titan* it gets darker and darker. I'm not really noticing what's around me—I'm just determined to keep up with Rick and Donny. I can hear Ralph and Joe making muffled cries as they hug my head, but I'm not stopping for anything.

Then!

Wow!

We have come out into a huge ball-room right in the middle of the *Titan*. The whole place is lit up, but I don't understand why. Then I look up to the ceiling. There's a hole in it and sunlight from the ocean surface is pouring in. I can see more collapsed decks above it leading up to massive smokestacks, bent over at crazy angles. They look like they've been caught in mid-fall by invisible hands. It looks really spooky! Although the middle of the ballroom is quite bright from the sun, the edges are covered in really dark shadow. Anything could be hiding there, waiting to pounce. . . .

Rick starts swimming around the ballroom, darting in and out of the seaweed-covered pillars. Then he starts doing barrel rolls and fin slides. He tail-flips into a double nosey and skims underneath me with a triple gill slap.

Show-off, I think.

"How cool is this place, and how cool am I?" shouts Rick as he shoots off again.

That's the final straw. It's time I show this show-off exactly what a hammer-head is capable of! Shaking Ralph and Joe clear, I speed off after Rick, knock-ing Donny right out of the way as I do.

Rick skids into a full tailspin. I give him

my best double gill flip. Rick just laughs in my face and is off again, tail-grinding along a handrail and single-finning across the hole between two torn-open rooms.

I follow. And then I make several mistakes, so many I can make a list of them.

1. I follow Rick without thinking—bad.
2. Not thinking means I don't measure the hole he goes through—bad, bad.
3. Not measuring the hole he goes through means I crash into the ragged gap in a half-twisty double-fin with pike—bad, bad, bad.
4. And I was probably traveling at twice my normal speed—bad beyond belief.

Creeeeeeeeeaaaaaaaaaaaakkkk!!!!

"That wasn't my rear!" I hear Joe shouting as I thud into the wall with a huge . . . thud.

I have just enough time to look up before the half-collapsed smokestacks above the ballroom start falling toward us with a horrible crashing, smashing, tearing, ripping sound.

And then everything goes dark!

CHAPTER 4

I think what happens next is this:

1. Donny crashes into Rick.

2. Rick crashes into me.

3. I crash into Joe.

4. Two of Joe's tentacles get stuck in my nostrils and
   I have to shake my head like crazy until my slimy
   jellyfish friend lets go.

The smokestack has crashed down over the hole in the ballroom ceiling, and nearly all the light is gone. I try to keep calm, but it's not easy. Especially when you've had jellyfish fingers stuck up your nose. But now that Joe has finally let go, I'm finding it easier to breathe. And I might not be able to see much, but I can still *hear* stuff.

I can hear someone's teeth chattering.

"Is everyone okay?" I ask.

"I want my mommy," says Joe.

"Me too!" says Donny.

"M-m-m-e-e thr-r-e-e-e," says some-one else.

"Ralph? Is that you?" I ask.

"N-n-n-n-no," says Rick. "It-it-it-it's me."

I'm shocked. Big, brave Rick the reef shark is so scared he can't keep his teeth still!

"Wh-wh-wh-what happened?" Rick asks.

"The smokestack fell down," I say.

"We need to get out of here!" yells Donny. "It's not safe! We'll be crushed!"

"He's r-r-r-r-right!" Rick says.

"Wait!" I start to say, but Donny is off. I feel him skim past me.

"No!" Donny calls back. "I'm going back out the way we—"

BOINNNNNNNNNNNG . . .

CREEEEEEEEEEEEEEEEEEEEEEAK . . .

CRASH!

I think these noises are:

1. Donny going *BOINNNNNNNNNNNG* as he bounces off a big metal door that has blocked the way we came in.
2. The vibration of the *BOINNNNNNNNNNNG* causing the smokestack to *CREEEEEEEEEEEEEEEAK* again.
3. The *CREEEEEEEEEEEEEEEEEEEEAK* of the smokestack causing a load of wood from the ceiling to *CRASH* down. Only just missing me, Joe, and Rick!

"Nobody move!" I shout. "We can't see anything, and every time we knock into something we make things even worse."

71

"Wh-wh-wh-wh-why are y-y-y-y-you s-s-s-suddenly in ch-ch-ch-ch-charge?" Rick chatters.

"Because my mouth isn't doing weird things with my teeth," I say.

"I-I-I-I-I-I'm   j-j-j-just c-c-c-c-cold," Rick whines. "That's all."

Yeah right, I think. But I don't say anything, because I have more important things to think about. Like where's Ralph?

"Where's Ralph?" I ask.

Silence.

"Ralph! Ralph!" I shout.

"He's probably dead," Joe says gloomily.

"I told you we'd be fish food if we came in here."

Silence.

POP.

"Joe!" Donny yells.

"Sorry," Joe mutters.

I swim around a bit, slowly and carefully. "Ralph? Are you okay?" But there's no sound apart from—

CREEEEEEEEEEEEEEEEEAK.

The wood and the smokestack shift again. But this time with no one bumping into anything. This is getting serious. We're trapped in a collapsing ship and I can't find my best friend! I clamp my jaw shut to stop *my* teeth from chattering with fear. I have to at least pretend to be brave or we'll never make it out.

"Okay, listen up, everyone, we've got to find Ralph and then we can get out of here."

"He's your f-f-f-friend, you f-f-f-find him!" says Rick. Donny just looks away.

I'm not going to get any help from the Terrified Twins, that's for sure.

I turn to look at Joe. He's wobbling his tentacles around in panic, mumbling,

"Fish food, If Not Exterminated. Why doesn't anyone ever listen to me?"

I'm beginning to wish I *had* listened to him.

There's nothing else I can do. I gulp and try not to look scared. "Right, you all stay here and I'll go and look for Ralph."

I kick my tail and swim off cautiously. My goggly eyes are a bit more used to the dark now, and I can start to make out some shapes. Lots of the ballroom's ceiling has come down all around us, but the huge rusty smokestack is lying right across the hole. You couldn't even fit a flatfish through the gap now. We are really, truly trapped.

I start to swim around in a circle, looking up and down, hoping that Ralph hasn't been hit by any of the falling wood. My heart is beating so hard I can feel it shaking my whole body.

From the other side of the ballroom Joe starts muttering again. "I reckon we're going to be stuck here so long we won't be home for dinner."

I swim alongside a pile of crushed chairs.

"In fact, we'll probably freeze to death before we ever get out."

I dart over broken, seaweed-covered tables.

"The only way I'm getting out of here is if some whale crashes his way in and wants a jellyfish ice pop."

I stick my head into a slimy fireplace. Still no Ralph.

"Or we'll get crushed up into plankton and eaten. Everyone will wonder where we've gone. They'll probably run a missing fish ad in the *Seaweed Times*, but it'll be too late. I just know we're not going to get out! I can sense it."

I'm just about to tell Joe to shut up, when something hits me like a wet fish in the face.

Sense it!

Joe said he could *sense* it.

Oh flibbery-flump! Of course. I can use my sensors to try to find Ralph. I quickly turn them on and start moving my hammerhead about, scanning the room. It's really faint, but I can definitely sense some movement coming from the other end of the ballroom. I swim off past Joe and I zoom in on the tiny vibration I can sense in my hammer.

BRRRRRMMMMMM.

As I reach the far end of the ballroom the vibration gets much stronger. It's not clear exactly where the vibration is coming from, but it's definitely around here somewhere.

I look left.

BRRRRrrrrrrrrmmmmmmmm . . .

I look right.

. . . mmmmMMMMBBBBRRRRRR!!!

I go right, and find a big wooden pillar. Underneath the pillar is a grand piano—one of those that has a big lid on top. It's standing all lopsided on broken legs. The lid is shut, and covered in pieces of the fallen ceiling. But what I see sticking out from the lid makes my hammerhead quiver. Waving slowly in the tiny opening is the bottom half of Ralph.

He's trapped inside the piano!

"Ralph! Ralph! It's me!" I shout.

"Harry?" Ralph squeaks from inside the piano. "Help! I can't move."

I rush forward and try to push the piano lid up with my fin.

It won't budge.

I flip around and shove my tail up against the wooden pillar that's on top. I push as hard as I can.

It won't budge either.

"Or maybe we'll get captured by leggy air-breathers who are doing research on the shipwreck, and no one will ever see us again," I hear Joe muttering from the other side of the room.

I take three swishes of my tail backward, turn and face the piano head-on, and leap toward it hammer-first. It hurts, but I manage to get the flat edge of my head into the opening beneath the piano lid.

I flick my tail harder and the lid creaks up a tiny bit, giving me enough room to slide my eye into the crack. I can see Ralph. He's on his side and still stuck, but he looks okay.

"Don't worry, Ralph," I say. "I'll have you out of here soon."

I can feel the weight of the pillar on the piano lid pressing onto my head, but I don't care. I've got to get Ralph out. But how? Maybe if I twisted my head sideways I'd be able to lift the lid higher.

I start kicking really hard with my tail fin.

The lid moves up a little.

I kick harder.

It moves up a little more.

I flap and flip my tail as hard as I can and twist my head until—

The lid springs up, tumbling the pillar onto the floor.

Ralph speeds out of the piano faster than a sailfish. I'm right behind him.

"Yaaaaaaaaaaaaaaaaaaaaaaaaaaaaaaay!" we both scream, high-finning each other and bumping chests.

"I thought I was never going to get out of there," Ralph gasps. "What happened?"

"Part of the ceiling caved in," I explain

as we swim back over to the others. "And a smokestack came down and blocked the hole."

We swim over to Joe, who is still sittting on the floor, hiding behind his tentacles.

"Look—I found Ralph!" I say.

Joe moves one of his tentacles and peeps out. But when he sees Ralph, he doesn't look happy.

"What's wrong?" I say.

"We're still doomed. Even if nothing happens to us, we'll still starve to death." Joe puts his tentacle back over his eyes.

Ralph and I roll *our* eyes. I look about and my heart sinks. "Where are Rick and Donny?"

"They said they weren't waiting for you to find Ralph and were going to smash their way out," Joe says.

CRAAAAAAAAAAAAAAAASH!!!!

"That must be them, then," says Joe.

Oh no!

I swim as fast as I can to the metal door. Rick and Donny are bashing themselves against it in a panic. I try to swim between Rick and the door. "Stop it!" I yell. "You'll bring the whole ship down on us!"

But Donny noses me out of the way

and Rick thuds into the door again.

There's nothing I can do to stop them.

"Look at the smokestack!" Ralph yells.

I look up. The smokestack is shifting again and the planks holding it up are beginning to give way. If we don't get out of here soon, we're fish cakes.

I dart back to Ralph and Joe. "Come on, let's try over there!" I point a fin to the far corner of the ballroom. Then I call back to Rick and Donny. "Come on, you two."

"You go if you w-w-w-want to!" Rick shouts at me. "But we're not moving. This is the way w-w-w-w-we came in, and this is the way we're going out. That way will just take you farther into the ship, and you'll be even more trapped."

I don't want to leave them, but if there's another way out I *have* to find it.

Joe, Ralph, and I swim along the wall, until we reach a jumbled pile of rotting furniture. We swim higher and higher up the pile, until, right at the top, we find a big sofa with springs popping out all over it, like a spiky puffer fish.

"Careful," I say to the other two as I dodge the springs. Once we've gotten past the pyramid of furniture, I can't believe my goggly eyes. There's a door!

And it doesn't seem to be blocked by anything. "Let's see where it goes," I call to the other two. "If it leads out of the ship, we can go and get Donny and Rick."

It's even colder on the other side of the doorway. We swim down a short, dark corridor, which opens onto a massive landing and a huge broken staircase as wide as a whale sandwich.

"Wow," I say.

Huge marble pillars have toppled down and smashed through the staircase. They look like a giant's fingers breaking through the wood.

Ralph and Joe start swimming around, looking for a way out, but there is only the staircase, which just seems to lead up to nowhere.

"Looks like we're stuck," says Ralph.

"Trapped in a watery grave," says Joe mournfully.

I swim to the bottom of the stairs and squint through the waving strands of seaweed and murky water. Then I catch sight of something.

"Yes!" I cry.

Up high, almost but not quite out of range of my hammerhead eyes, I can see a tiny glimmer of light. I swivel my eyes and focus them as hard as I can. There, high above us, in the roof of the *Titan*, is a skylight. It's been smashed, and through it I can see a beam of sunlight in the water.

It's a way out!

We're saved!

Or we would have been. But that's when the whole ship begins to shake and rumble, and the hugest *CRASH!!!* yet comes from the direction of the ballroom.

CHAPTER 5

Ralph, Joe, and I burst back into the ballroom and find the water churning up like a
whirlpool, full of dust and bits of wood.

"Rick!" I call. "Donny! Are you okay?"
But there's no answer. "Split up," I say to
Ralph and Joe. "We've got to find them
and get up those stairs."

"Okay," Ralph says.

Joe is fishing pieces of dirt out of his mouth with his tentacles. "Mmmph mmmph we'll be exploded into jelly beans mmmph," he says.

"Come on!" I say.

We all swim off in different directions. I head for the metal door, and just when I think the day can't get any worse, it does.

Donny is swimming in circles by the door, crying and shaking.

"Where's Rick?" I say.

Donny slowly points a trembling fin behind me.

I turn and squint through the murky water. And see Rick trapped inside a glittery gold cage. I can hardly believe my eyes. So I blink them. Then I swivel them. But I wasn't seeing things—Rick really is trapped inside a glittery gold cage.

What I think happened is this:

1. Donny and Rick kept smashing into the door.
   (NOT GOOD.)
2. The vibrations they caused traveled up through the ship until they reached the ceiling.
   (NOT GOODER.)
3. This shook one of the enormous chandeliers so much that it crashed down on top of Rick and trapped him on the floor. **(NOT GOODER-ER!)**

"Get me out," Rick wails.

RUUUUUUUUUUMMMMMBLE!

The whole ship vibrates. Clouds of splinters puff out from the beams above us like coral blooms. The ballroom is about to collapse completely. Ralph and Joe swim over in a panic.

"Don't just float there! Get me out!" Rick yells.

Donny is still swimming around and around in circles. I grab him by the fins. "Donny! We need your help. We won't be able to get Rick out on our own."

Donny's eyes are filled with tears, and his bottom lip is trembling. "You don't even like Rick, so why would you want to help him?"

"Well, I wouldn't leave him here to get crushed, would I?"

Donny sniffs. "I guess not."

"Good, now are you going to help us or what?"

Donny nods, and I pat him on the fin.

"Get me out!" Rick screams.

"Right," I say, trying to sound like I know what I'm doing and I have a plan, which I don't. "Ummmm . . ."

The chandelier is massive. The gold rails are all bent over in arches. There are lots of little rings attached, which were probably used for glass jewels or something, but now they're just empty. These rings are what I'm *really* interested in.

Now I have a plan!

"Okay, everyone wedge your fin into a ring on this side of the chandelier," I say.

No one moves.

Joe opens his mouth to speak, but I cut him off.

"No, we're not going to freeze to death, or become ice pops and eaten by whales, or get turned into plankton, or get featured in the *Seaweed Times*, or get captured by leggy air-breathers, or starve to death, or explode into jelly beans. At least, we won't if you *hurry up!*" I say.

"No, it's not that," Joe says.

"What is it, then?" I ask.

"GET ME OUT!" Rick yells.

"What if you don't have a fin?" Joe asks.

"Oh! Well, use your strongest tentacles," I say.

RUUUUUUUUUUMMMMMBLE!

"Now!" I shout. "We don't have time to be scared!"

I wriggle my right fin up into a ring and shove my dorsal fin against it. The others do the same, but I can see the fear in their faces as they all look over at me to show that they're ready.

This had better work.

"Rick—get ready to swim out, okay?" I say.

"Just hurry up!" Rick yells.

"Okay, everyone!" I shout. "Swim up now!"

I kick with my tail. Ralph and Donny do the same. Joe does something complicated with his tentacles.

The chandelier shifts a tiny bit, but not enough!

"Get me out!"

CRRRRREEEEEEEEEAAAAAKKKKKK!!!

This is our last chance!

"One . . . ," I count.

"Two . . ."

Joe's bottom toots.

"Three!"

I kick and kick and kick my tail, harder than I ever have before.

The chandelier starts to move.

"Keep going!" I shout.

Kick.

Kick.

Kick. Kick. Kick!

The chandelier lurches upward. Rick flattens himself against the floor and slides underneath the edges of the cage. He's out!

"Okay, let go!" I yell.

We all swim away and the chandelier crashes back to the floor.

"Follow me," I say, swimming for the doorway leading to the staircase. We zoom across the deck, up over the pile of wrecked furniture, past the springs of the busted sofa, and out through the door into the dark corridor. I can hear the others flapping behind me. I turn to make sure everyone is through the door okay. Rick, Donny, Ralph, and then Joe, puffing up behind. Jellyfish aren't exactly built for speed, but he's doing a great job.

"Everyone up the stairs. Up to the skylight. Come on!"

We race up the stairs toward the skylight

and burst out of the roof like corks from a bottle, whooping and high-finning each other like crazy. Down below us there is a final **RUUUUUUUUUUMMMMMMBLE** as the *Titan* collapses like a seashell being squashed by a giant fin!

CHAPTER 6

I don't think I've ever seen Mrs. Shelby look so happy. She's smiling wide enough to swallow a baby whale.

"Harry! Ralph! Joe! Donny! Rick!" she calls to us. "Oh my goodness, I've been so worried!"

We swim down to the seabed, where

Mrs. Shelby has gathered the class together out of danger. All the kids look pretty scared of the noises coming from the *Titan*. Not only is Penny Puffer-Fish still spiky, but all the hermit-crab kids have gone right inside their shells and shut the doors.

We skid to a halt in front of the class, me doing a triple nosey and the best gill grind ever.

"We thought you were trapped inside!" Mrs. Shelby says, hugging each of us. She probably hugs Joe just a little bit too tight, because he toots again, but she doesn't seem to mind.

I'm just about to tell her everything
that happened, when a fin slaps onto
my face and covers my mouth so I
can't speak. The fin belongs to Rick.
He pushes in front of me. "Well, Mrs.
Shelby, if I hadn't gotten everyone out,

we might not have made it at all. Right, Donny?"

I stare so hard at Rick that it feels like my eyes might pop out of my hammerhead. I can't believe what he's saying. Just a couple of minutes ago he was shrieking for help, stuck under a chandelier.

"I tried to tell them not to go into the *Titan*, Mrs. Shelby, but they wouldn't listen," Rick continues. "And I couldn't just let them go in alone, could I?"

I glance at Ralph and Joe. They look just as annoyed as I am. We're all so annoyed, we can't get any words out!

This is so unfair. I start to open my mouth to complain, but then all the kids in the class start laughing. Great! So now not only do they think I've got a weird hammerhead, they think I'm reckless, too. But as I swivel my eyes around I notice that the rest of the class is all pointing and laughing at Rick. As he swims around in front of Mrs. Shelby I see something glinting and sparkling on his back. Some jewels from the chandelier have gotten caught on his dorsal fin like a princess's tiara.

He looks ridiculous.

I begin laughing too, so hard I end up doing three barrel rolls. By the time I finish, Mrs. Shelby is waving her big flippers to calm the class down and Rick is just floating there with a bright red face.

"What are you all laughing at?" he whines.

Ha! Now that he knows what it feels like, maybe he won't flubber my head so much in the future. Win!

Ralph swims past me and turns to the class. "We wouldn't have gotten out of there if it wasn't for Harry, Mrs. Shelby," he says. "It was Rick who wanted to go into the *Titan*, not Harry. When the smokestack collapsed and everything went dark, I got trapped inside a piano and it was Harry and his hammerhead sensors that got me out. Rick was too busy trying to save his own skin. Harry is the bravest shark in the whole sea."

I feel my hammerhead turning coral

pink as the whole class looks from Rick's tiara to me. I don't really like being the center of attention—even if it's for a good thing. But Ralph keeps going. "And when Rick got trapped under a chandelier, it was Harry who showed us how to get him out, and it was Harry's awesome hammerhead eyes that found the way out through the skylight. All Rick did while we were in there was show off and cry."

Everyone in the class is staring open-mouthed at me. Even Mrs. Shelby. I don't know what to say.

Mrs. Shelby closes her mouth, thinks

for a moment, then calls Rick and me forward. "You two boys are very, very naughty for disobeying me and going into the *Titan*. If you'd listened to me, none of this would have happened, and none of you would have been in any danger at all. Do you understand?"

We both nod. This makes Rick's tiara sparkle, and the three angelfish behind us giggle under their breath.

"Really, I should punish you all for going into the ship," Mrs. Shelby continues, "but since Harry has been so brave, and he managed to bring you all back to safety, I'll let you off the hook.

But just this once, understand?"

The class cheers and claps. Ralph and Joe swim up to me and we high-fin and high-tentacle.

Donny swims off to one side with Rick, and I watch as he whispers in his ear, telling him about the tiara. Rick twists and turns his pointy face, trying to get a look at his fin.

"Get it off me!" he yells at Donny.

Donny pulls at the jewels with his teeth and Rick twists some more. But the jewels are stuck tight and the sharks' struggles only make the class laugh even louder. Donny and Rick look like they are dancing together in that really embarrassing way that moms and dads do.

Mrs. Shelby calms the class down all over again. Then we set off back to school. As we go I make my final list of the day—of all the good things that have happened:

1. Everyone is safe. *(Genius.)*
2. Rick's tiara incident is going to keep him from

picking on me for a while. *(Super genius!)*

3. What started out as the worst day ever has turned into the best day ever! *(More-super-than-Rick's-tiara genius!)*

Being a hammerhead might not be so bad after all. . . .

THE END

Meet Harry and the Shark Point gang. . . .

HARRY

Species:

hammerhead shark

You'll spot him . .

using his special

hammer-vision

Favorite thing:

his Gregor the Gnasher

poster

Most likely to say:

"I wish I was a great white."

Most embarrassing moment: when Mom called him

her "little starfish" in front of all his friends

RALPH

Species:

pilot fish

You'll spot him . . .

eating the food

from between

Harry's teeth!

Favorite thing: shrimp Pop-Tarts

Most likely to say: "So, Harry, what's for

breakfast today?"

Most embarrassing moment: eating too much cake

on Joe's birthday. His face was COVERED in pink

plankton icing.

JOE

Species: jellyfish

You'll spot him . . . hiding behind Ralph and Harry, or behind his own tentacles

Favorite thing: his cave, since it's nice and safe

Most likely to say: "If we do this, we're going to end up as fish food. . . ."

Most embarrassing moment: whenever his rear goes *toot*, which is when he's scared. Which is all the time.

RICK

Species: blacktip reef
shark

You'll spot him . . .
bullying smaller fish
or showing off

Favorite thing: his

black leather jacket

Most likely to say: "Last one there's a sea snail!"

Most embarrassing moment:

none. Rick's far too cool to get embarrassed.

SHARK BITES

Sharks have been swimming in the world's oceans for more than 400 million years.

There are more than four hundred different species of shark, from the giant hammerhead to the goblin shark.

Sharks do not have bones. They are cartilaginous fish, which means their skeletons are made of cartilage, not bone. Cartilage is a type of connective tissue that is softer than bone. Humans have cartilage in their ears and nose.

The shortfin mako is the fastest shark in the ocean. It can swim in bursts as fast as forty-six miles per hour.

The whale shark is the largest shark in the sea. It can grow to be as long as sixty feet.

122

HAMMERHEADS

There are nine species of hammerhead shark, including scoophead and bonnethead.

A wild hammerhead can live for twenty to thirty years.

Hammerheads live in moderate and tropical warm waters.

The largest hammerhead is the great hammerhead, which can weigh about five hundred pounds.

The eyes of the hammerhead shark, which are on each side of its head, allow the hammerhead to look around an area more quickly than other sharks. It also has special sensors across its head that help it scan for food.

Hammerheads eat stingrays, bony fish, crabs, lobsters, squid, and many other sea creatures.